≠
V862m

MY TWIN SISTER ERIKA

MY TWIN SISTER
ERIKA

by ILSE-MARGRET VOGEL

Harper & Row, Publishers
New York, Hagerstown, San Francisco, London

To Howard, my second twin,
and with special thanks to
Charlotte and Nina,
the godmothers of this book.

Contents

MY TWIN SISTER ERIKA

Who Is Who?

"Today I will be you," my twin sister Erika said, snatching the red hair ribbon out of my hand before I could put it on. "Here, you take my blue ribbon."

"No," I said, trying to get my ribbon back. "Today I will be me. I was you yesterday and the day before yesterday, and the day before the day before yesterday. Today I will be Inge. Today I will be myself."

Erika shook her head. "What's the good of

being yourself?" she said. "Isn't it more fun to know you are Inge and yet make everyone think you are Erika all day long?"

"Well," I said, "it's fun when we fool Uncle Max. It's fun when he can't tell us apart."

"Besides," Erika went on, "Erika is a much nicer name than Inge. You should be happy I let you be me."

This was true. Erika always sounded so much better to me than my own name. Out of E-RI-KA one could make a little song. The *E* and the *I* and the *A* were so musical. But IN-GE! The *G* in the middle of my name ruined the whole sound. It was like a rock.

"All right?" Erika asked. "All right?" She giggled as she tied my red ribbon in her blond hair.

Since I had not really said yes, she went on, "Because you are Erika again today, you can play with Fat-Belly-Cross-Eye."

Fat-Belly-Cross-Eye was a plump, little curly-haired boy doll dressed like the mountain people of Tyrol. Uncle Max had given him to Erika only yesterday. His blue eyes did not stare straight ahead but moved in slightly toward his nose. "Fat-Belly-Cross-Eye will be his name,"

2

Erika had said when she saw him. For me Uncle Max had brought a doll with long, golden braids of real hair. *Real*, real hair. They were the kind of braids I had always wanted myself, but my hair was too thin. The doll wore a pink dress and patent leather shoes, and I named her Frieda.

Fat-Belly-Cross-Eye was our very first boy doll, and Erika had scarcely let me touch him. So I said, "All right."

"And you will let me play with Frieda," asked Erika, "and let me comb her hair, too?"

"All right," I said, and I tied Erika's blue ribbon in my hair. Then I put on my dress, which matched Erika's as always.

Together we stepped in front of the mirror. I saw two faces that were exactly alike. So alike, I had to make a funny face to find out which one I was. But the other face made a funny face, too. So I had to look at the blue ribbon to see which face was mine.

We went downstairs. Uncle Max was sitting at the breakfast table with a big newspaper in front of him.

"Good morning, Uncle Max," I said.

"Good morning, good morning. Who are you?"

he asked from behind his paper. "Well—let me see," he said without looking. "I think I know. I think you are Inge. Now, let me *really* see."

I was disappointed at being recognized, but only for a second, because when Uncle Max lowered his paper and saw the blue ribbon in my hair, he chuckled.

"I did it again. I thought I could recognize you by your voice, but now I see you are Erika." And turning to Erika, he said, "Good morning, Inge."

"Good morning, Uncle Max."

"Come, sit down," Uncle Max said. "Your mother and grandmother have gone to the market, your father to his office, and I am here to see that you eat a good breakfast."

Erika sat down on Uncle Max's right, and I sat down on his left. We held in our giggles and exchanged glances. We loved Uncle Max. He came to our house twice a year and always brought us presents. He showed us card tricks and other bits of magic. He could stand a coin on its side and make it roll up his arm, uphill all the way, from his wrist to his forearm. Then he would make the coin disappear and a moment later lift it out of Erika's hair or my ear. We loved Uncle Max, and we loved to fool him when we could.

Now Uncle Max looked at the porridge in front of us and reached for the bowl of stewed fruit.

"This will help the porridge," he said, smiling. "An apricot for Erika and an apricot for Inge. A plum for Erika and a plum for Inge. An apricot for . . ." He kept this up until there was only one plum left in the bowl. "Who shall have the last one?" he asked.

Quickly I said, "It's for me because I'm the oldest."

"Yes," Uncle Max said, "that is true. You, Erika, are half an hour older than your twin sister Inge."

"No, no," interrupted Erika. "Erika is a *day* older than Inge."

"No, no, just half an hour," I insisted.

"No," Erika said, "a day older. A whole day older!"

"No, you aren't," I screamed. "You're just half an hour older." By now I was so angry, I couldn't keep track of who was who and who was allowed to say what.

"Now, now, no fighting, no screaming," Uncle

Max said gently. "You are both right. Erika was born on June fourth, just fifteen minutes before midnight. Inge arrived fifteen minutes past midnight on June fifth. A day later on the calendar but just half an hour of life."

"Yes, yes, just half an hour," I burst out. I had completely forgotten the blue ribbon in my hair, which obliged me to be Erika. "She is only half an hour older than I am and she *always* orders me about." My cheeks were wet with tears.

Uncle Max took out his handkerchief and dabbed my face. Then, bringing his eyes close to mine, he touched the ridge of my nose with his forefinger. "You are *Inge*," he said. "You have no blue vein over your nose like your sister Erika. And since you are the baby in the family, you will get the extra plum."

Magda's Best Friend

Erika was born with a thin, pale blue vein over the ridge of her nose. To people who did not know this, we looked exactly the same. And people who knew had to look very close to see it. Only then could they tell who was Erika and who was Inge.

Magda, the girl who lived next door, was one person who knew. Just the same, she was glad when Mother began the blue-ribbon-Erika, red-ribbon-Inge arrangement. Not that we would ever want to fool Magda. It would have been easy, but neither of us wanted to upset her even a little bit. We adored her. She was a year older than we were, and when she was willing to play with us, we were in heaven.

I was in the garden after breakfast, waiting and hoping Magda would come out. When at last she appeared, I called, "Hello, Magda." And to save her the trouble of having to ask who I was, I said immediately, "I'm Inge."

"Where is Erika?" she asked, walking slowly toward the iron fence that separated her garden from ours.

"She is inside," I said, and quickly added, "and she doesn't want to come out."

This was a lie. I knew very well that Erika would drop anything if Magda asked for her. But I was hoping to keep Magda for myself all morning.

"Why don't you go and ask her to come over?" Magda said. "You both can help me pick raspberries."

I didn't dare *not* to do as Magda wished, so I went into the house. But once inside, I tiptoed past the room where Erika was playing. I picked up Frieda, the doll Uncle Max had given me, and holding my breath, I tiptoed out again.

"Where is Erika?" Magda asked when I came to the fence.

"She can't come," I answered, and quickly shoved Frieda through the bars of the fence into Magda's hands. "You can play with Frieda," I bubbled on. "You can undo her braids. She has real hair. *Real* hair. See?"

Magda took Frieda and looked at her. She laid her flat on her back to see if her eyes would close. The eyelids with long, beautiful lashes—real hair, too—did close. Then Magda lifted Frieda's pink dress and looked at the white petticoat edged with lace. The panties under the petticoat had the same pretty lace. The black patent leather shoes could be removed, and Magda took them off. She ran her hand over the white, silky stockings.

Magda nodded her head and smiled, which made me a very proud doll mother.

"You can untie the ribbons on Frieda's braids," I said. "I'll come over and show you." As fast as I could, I ran up our garden path to the heavy iron gate, ran to Magda's open gate and ran down Magda's garden path. She was still in the same spot next to the fence, with Frieda on her lap. She had undone both braids, and Frieda's glittering golden hair spilled down to her knees.

How I loved that long, long hair. How much I wished for braids myself. And so did Erika. But Mother would never listen to us. Every few weeks our hair was trimmed to look like page boys' hair.

Magda stroked Frieda's hair and said, "I want to comb her hair. Do you have a comb, Inge?"

"No," I answered.

"Go get one," Magda ordered.

And I did. Running fast, I hurried along the path. I entered the house silently, took a comb from our bedroom and tiptoed out again. I arrived back at Magda's breathless. By now she had taken all of Frieda's clothes off. "I am going to give her a completely new hairdo," she said. "All right?"

"All right," I said, "but let's move over behind the bushes in the shade." Not that I wanted shade. The morning was cool and the sun felt good. I wanted us to be hidden.

Erika, who by now must have wondered where I was, might soon come looking for me.

It was wonderful to have Magda all for myself. Frieda took most of her attention, but I was not jealous. After all, Frieda was only a doll and could not talk. If Erika had been there, she would have been doing all the talking. There would have been no chance for me to say a word.

But Magda did not want to move. She was busy combing Frieda's hair. I began to tell her about Uncle Max. I was in the middle of describing his wonderful card tricks when the terrible thing happened—

Erika stood in front of me. Magda and I had been too busy to see her approach. My wonderful twosomeness with Magda was over.

I felt my cheeks get hot. "Erika, I wish you were dead!" burst out of me.

"But I *like* Erika," said Magda, still combing Frieda's hair.

Erika paid no attention to me or what I had said, so I repeated, "I wish you were dead!"

"No," said Magda, turning to me for a second. "Erika is my best friend."

"And I? Who am I?" My voice trembled.

"You are my friend," said Magda, without raising her eyes from Frieda.

"I thought *I* was your best friend," I pleaded. "Once you told me so. Am I? Am I?"

"Well, sometimes," said Magda in a cool voice.

"When is sometimes?" I wanted to know.

But Magda did not hear me. Instead she was listening to Erika tell about the new doll Uncle Max had given her.

"He's tremendous and wonderful and marvelous," said Erika. "He's called Fat-Belly-Cross-Eye and he's a boy."

Magda got interested. "Inge, go fetch him," she said.

And I did. But I didn't run this time. Slowly I walked back to our house, picked up Erika's doll and returned just as slowly.

Magda glanced at Fat-Belly-Cross-Eye, said "Nice," and continued to comb Frieda's hair.

Now Erika looked hurt. "Frieda might have long hair—" she began.

"*Real*, long hair," I interrupted.

"—but my Fat-Belly-Cross-Eye is much nicer. Look, Magda, look at his pink cheeks and his blue eyes, just a little bit cross-eyed. Look at

15

his curly hair under his hat. It's a real Tyrolean hat!"

Magda took Fat-Belly-Cross-Eye in her hands and looked him over.

"See how he's dressed," said Erika, "just the way they dress in the mountains of Tyrol. And you know what, Magda? Since you are my best friend, you can keep him all day today and even overnight."

Magda nodded and accepted. She got up and carried Fat-Belly-Cross-Eye into her house. Erika followed her. My Frieda was left lying in the grass, undressed. Her half-combed hair covered her face.

I picked Frieda up, hugged her and carried her home. Then I put her clothes back on and began to comb her hair. I would make up a new hairdo, I decided. It would be the best hairdo ever. But time and again I stopped combing. I walked up to the second floor, hoping I could spy on Magda and Erika from the hall window. I couldn't see them anywhere. After a while I went down to the back porch and heard their laughter.

I couldn't see them, but from the sound of

a ball bouncing off a wall, I knew they were playing Ten Kings. I started to walk along the fence, whistling loudly, trying to make myself heard. After a while they heard me. Magda looked around from behind some bushes and called, "Come over, Inge. We're playing ball." This time I ran. When I arrived, they were adding up their scores.

Magda stopped counting, pointed to a basket and said, "Inge, you can start picking raspberries. My mother is waiting for them."

I just stood there. I would have loved to play ball with them. I was very good at playing Ten Kings, and I wanted Magda to see how good I was.

"What are you waiting for?" Magda asked. "Go on, pick berries. We'll come soon."

I walked over to the berry patch. After all, it was better to pick berries for Magda than not be close to her at all. Besides, I wanted to do things for her, so that I might become her best friend again.

The basket was nearly full when Magda and Erika joined me. It was Erika who carried the full basket to Magda's mother. And it was

Erika who got all the thank-yous and a handful of candy. She gave three candies to Magda, two to herself and one to me.

That night I couldn't fall asleep for a long time. What could I do to make myself Magda's best friend again? It would have to be something so grand that Erika could not possibly match it. I thought and thought, but I could think of nothing.

In the morning the first thing Erika said was that she missed Fat-Belly-Cross-Eye and should never have let Magda keep him overnight. She said we should ask for him back right after breakfast.

We ate our oats as fast as we could, ran to the back porch and called for Magda. After what seemed a long while, Magda opened a window to shout back she had no time. Then she shut the window.

Erika got very quiet. Half an hour later she came to me and said she had hardly slept at all the night before because she had missed Fat-Belly-Cross-Eye terribly. She wanted me to go over to Magda's to get him. She said if I did, I could have her doll carriage for a whole week and she wouldn't even ask me to let her have my doll cradle.

"Please go get him right now," Erika begged. She looked as if she were going to cry.

"All right," I said. I didn't argue because I felt sorry for her. Also, I had an idea.

I took Frieda under my arm and went over to Magda's. She was still eating breakfast. Fat-Belly-Cross-Eye was on her lap.

"Magda," I said, "Erika wants him back. She wants him back right now."

"Right now?" said Magda. "We aren't even through with breakfast. What's the matter with Erika?"

"Well," I said, "that's the way she is. She wants him back. Right now."

I waited, saying nothing, just watching Magda. I kept Frieda behind my back. When Magda began to look unhappy, I pushed Frieda into her lap.

"You can have my Frieda for a whole week," I said. "Day and night. And you can do to her whatever you want."

"Fine," said Magda, "that's fine." And she handed me Fat-Belly-Cross-Eye.

19

The week that followed was very long. Every day I filled Erika's doll buggy with all my dolls and pushed them around. When I got tired of that, I took out the dolls and decided to move stones from one end of the garden to the other. Erika caught me but was mad only because I had forgotten to take the white pillows and the lace cover out of the buggy. I put back the dolls, but it wasn't really fun. None of the dolls had Frieda's beautiful hair, Frieda's real hair. None of them had hair that could be combed and braided and combed again.

I didn't see Magda all that week. She kept to herself in her own house. The morning the week was over, I rushed to Magda's before breakfast and asked for Frieda.

"Has it been a week already?" Magda asked in surprise.

"Yes," I said. "I've crossed off every day on the calendar since last Monday. Did you like having Frieda?"

"Yes, I had fun," Magda answered. "I'll go get her now." And slowly, very slowly, she left the room.

She stayed away a long time.

When she came back, my heart beat fast at the

first sight of Frieda's face. Magda had wrapped a pretty silk-like scarf around Frieda's head. She said I could keep the scarf because Frieda looked so nice in it.

"Yes, she does, she does," I said. "Oh, thank you, Magda."

I took Frieda and pressed her to my heart. I hugged and kissed her so hard, the scarf slipped off her head. It slipped off and—I looked and I couldn't believe my eyes.

Frieda's hair had been cut! Cut as short as mine. As short as Erika's.

I stared at Frieda, then at Magda.

"She looks nice with hair like yours, doesn't she?" said Magda, putting her arm around my shoulder.

I couldn't answer.

"Doesn't she?" Magda insisted.

"No," I stammered, "no, she does not." And half against my will I asked, "How could you do it?"

"Well," said Magda, "you told me I could do anything I wanted with her. And after I had given her all the hairdos I could think of, I wanted to see what she would look like with short hair. And she does look nice—she does!"

For a while I couldn't speak. I tried to hold back my tears. Then I said, "Magda, am I your best friend now?"

Magda looked puzzled.

"Am I?" I asked again.

Magda smiled, shrugged her shoulders and said, "Sometimes."

Erika's Secret

"I have a plan and you must help me," Erika said early one morning.

"No thank you," I said. "I have my own plans for today."

"Too bad," Erika said, "because I know you would love my plan."

"You don't know what I love," I answered. "I certainly do not love being ordered about all the time, which is just what would happen if I would help you."

"All right," said Erika, "all right. But I know you will be sorry if you can't move in with me."

"Move in where?"

"Won't tell you," said Erika, and she left the room.

It was not true that I had my own plans for the day. I had no plan at all. "I wish I knew Erika's plan," I said to Frieda.

When we met at breakfast, I said, "Erika, tell me your plan. Please."

"Will you help?" she asked.

I knew what it meant to help her. It meant that she would stand and frown, put her hand to her chin and say, "Let me think." Then, after she'd be through thinking, she would say, "Go get this." Or, "Go do that."

"No," I said, "I won't help you."

"All right," said Erika. "Since my plan is very secret, you are not allowed to follow me. You must stay here, close your eyes and count to one hundred before you leave the house. And you cannot go into the garden behind the house. It will take me all day, maybe longer, doing it all by myself. But when it is finished, it will belong to me—all to me myself."

"What will belong all to you yourself?"

Erika grinned, then asked, "Will you go get me a hammer and a saw?"

By now I was very curious. Erika needed a hammer; she needed a saw. I said, "Maybe you need some nails, too."

"Yes," Erika said, "get us some nails, too."

I went to the basement, where Father kept his tools, and came back with a hammer, a saw and a box of nails. Erika had a ruler and some pencils.

"I have a good long rope," I said. "Do you want it?"

"Yes," said Erika, "one never knows."

When Erika saw how much there was to carry —hammer, saw, nail box, rope—she was happy to have my help.

"Nobody must see where we go," Erika whispered. "We want to go to the far end of the garden. But in case someone should see us, we will leave by the front door. To mislead them." I nodded. Sometimes Erika was very smart.

We left by the front door. Under cover of the pines and bushes along the west side of the house, we half-walked, half-crept until we reached the end of the garden. There was a small gate, usually locked, but the day before

Erika had found it open. Beyond the gate was a little brook edged with willows and birches.

"Put everything down here," Erika ordered.

Then, with a grand gesture, she pointed across the brook and said, "We will build a house here."

"A house?" I asked.

"Yes," said Erika, "a house for hiding."

As wonderful as this sounded, I could not see how we could build a house. I said so.

"Look," said Erika, "everything is here. See these four trees? Just perfect. And one chair is here already. I've figured it all out. You'll see."

All I saw were trees, many more than four, and a tree stump.

"Of course, we need a few boards," Erika said. "There are some behind the chicken coop. Come, we'll get them."

We picked the best from the pile of old boards. "Nine will do," said Erika. Nine, I thought. How could she know that?

We carried back the nine boards to the place where, Erika said, we were going to build a house. We began to nail the boards to the trees. Erika knew exactly where and how. It was hard work. The boards were heavy, and the second and third rows higher up were a struggle. When all nine boards were nailed to the four trees, I still couldn't imagine how this could become a house, but I didn't dare say so. Then Grandmother's faraway voice called us in for lunch.

We ate little and we ate fast. We dashed out again as soon as possible.

"Now we need two long sticks to hold the roof," said Erika.

"The roof?" I asked.

"A house has to have a roof," said Erika. We searched for sticks along the brook until we found two. I had to hold them as high as I could, and Erika nailed them to the trees. One in front and one in back.

Then Erika stepped back to inspect what she called a house "It's fine," she said. "It will be just grand. All we need now is a blanket. You go and ask Grandmother for the old blanket she carried to the attic the other day."

"Why me?" I said. "Why can't you ask her?"

"Because," said Erika, "you are her favorite! You are the baby. She will give it to you."

Ten minutes later I was back with the big green blanket. Erika did not say thank-you; she only said "Fine." She threw the blanket over the back stick, and together we tried to bring it forward to the front stick. It didn't work. Time and again the blanket slipped off the back stick.

Now she's stuck, I thought, and I hoped that *I* would come up with an idea. But before I could even begin to concentrate, Erika smiled and said, "I know. Get the rope you brought." We cut the rope into small pieces. There were moth holes at one end of the blanket, and Erika pulled the pieces of rope through them and tied the blanket to the back stick. Now we could pull the blanket forward and make it fall over the front stick. Now we had a roof and a door for the house.

I had to admit Erika was wonderful.

Erika smiled. "Let's go inside," she said. Quickly she sat down on the only chair. I sat next to her on the ground. It was beautiful! Our very own house with a little brook at our doorstep. For a long time we sat and gazed at the moving water without saying a word.

Then Grandmother called us for afternoon cookies. Hand in hand we walked back to the house.

"What have you been up to?" asked Grand-

mother as we approached. "You both look so happy."

I was happy until Erika whispered, "Don't tell! Don't tell anybody about my house. It's a secret. Understand?"

I nodded. I understood. I also understood that it was *her* house.

But I still went with Erika to the house in the days that followed. Every day she thought of improvements. We added sticks and branches to the boards to make the walls more solid. We tied the hanging blanket to one of the front trees to widen the entrance door. I found a tin can and filled it with beautiful wild flowers. We made new plans and changed them and made still better plans.

Then one day Erika put up a sign at the entrance tree:

ERIKA'S SECRET HOUSE

I was so hurt, I turned my back and left. After that I didn't go to the house anymore. For several days we hardly talked to each other. I stayed in the front garden. Erika was alone in *her* house.

Soon it was June and our birthdays came around. We still weren't talking much, but a birthday is a birthday, and my heart softened. I picked out one of Frieda's best dresses to give to Erika for her doll Lora. And to make it really special, I added a wide, red velvet ribbon as a sash. Erika had wanted that ribbon for a long time.

Mother and Grandmother always set up a birthday table for us. A long garland of marguerites and cornflowers edged the table on which the presents were arranged. In the middle there was always the wooden ring which held the candles. Eight candles this time, and in the center, the thick Life Candle. After Erika had seen all her presents and kissed and thanked Mother, Father and Grandmother, she turned to kiss me. I had not given her my present yet. I had kept it behind my back. I wanted her to see my present last.

When I held out the dress with the red velvet sash, Erika got very excited.

"Oh, Inge," she said, "Lora wanted this dress so much. It's just beautiful with the red velvet ribbon." I was surprised at how hard she hugged and kissed me.

The next day would be my birthday, and there would be presents for me on the flower-edged table. Erika woke me early, urging me to go to the secret house with her.

I shook my head no.

"You *must* come and see all the wonderful things I've done to it," Erika insisted. "You must." And she took my arm and pulled me with her.

It was a beautiful morning with singing birds, a perfect birthday day. I was curious to see the house again, but the closer we came to the end of the garden, the slower I walked.

Finally I said, "I want to go back. It's *my* birthday, and I don't want to look at *your* house."

"Oh, come on," said Erika. *"Please,* Inge."

I don't know, it must have been the way she said "please" that made me follow her. Erika swung open the gate and pushed me ahead.

"There," she said, and she began to sing "Happy Birthday."

There was a new sign on the entrance tree. In big letters it said:

INGE'S SECRET HOUSE

Magda, the Guest of Honor

Magda had been away for several days and had not seen our secret house. We waited eagerly for her return.

"When she comes back, we will have a welcome party in your secret house," said Erika.

"That will be wonderful," I said, "and we will decorate it and make it look even more beautiful."

"How can we make a comfortable seat for Magda?" Erika asked. "We can't let her sit on the ground."

"Why not?" I said. "I always sit on the ground."

"Because she is our guest of honor," Erika answered, "and besides . . . because she is Magda."

I remembered seeing two short tree logs at the bend in the brook. With great effort we rolled them into the back corner of our secret house.

"The wall will be the back of the chair," said Erika, "so Magda can lean against it comfortably."

Erika tried sitting on the logs and decided they were not comfortable enough yet.

"At least not for Magda," she said.

"I can get the pillows from your doll buggy and my doll cradle," I suggested.

"Good," said Erika. So I got them.

"Much better," Erika said, sitting down on the pillow-covered logs.

"I'll make a garland of wild flowers to hang at the entrance," I said. "Erika, you know how to make such nice signs. Can you make a welcome sign for Magda?"

Erika went back to the house, and I picked marguerites and bluebells in the meadow. I was only halfway through braiding the long garland when Erika came back with a large cardboard sign saying:

WELCOME HOME MAGDA

Each letter was big and bold, and each was a different color. The sign was beautiful.

"How could you do that so fast?" I asked.

"Well," said Erika, "I *am* an artist."

When Magda returned, we hung the welcome sign and the garland. Then we went to Magda's house to invite her over for the afternoon. Erika made mysterious remarks about a welcome party in a secret house.

"All right," said Magda, "I will come at three o'clock." At three o'clock sharp she arrived.

In great excitement we walked her to the end of our garden. Approaching the secret house, we stood back and waited, letting Magda go ahead of us.

But she did not stop and gasp in surprise, as we had hoped. She stepped over the little brook as if it weren't there, looked briefly at Erika's sign and my garland, and went inside.

We hurried after her. "Please sit down," said Erika, with a sweeping gesture of her arm. "This is your chair."

Magda flopped down on the pillows.

"Lean back," Erika urged, "lean back and enjoy the view."

But Magda did not lean back. Instead she hunched forward, resting her elbows on her knees, and made a face.

"What's the matter?" I asked. "Don't you like it?"

"Well," said Magda, "it's *so* uncomfortable."

Erika was sitting on her tree stump, and I sat on the ground. We did not know what to say and were thankful when a large black-and-yellow butterfly went sailing past.

"Beautiful," Erika whispered. "Isn't it beautiful, Magda?"

"I have seen bigger ones," said Magda.

Erika and I looked at each other, trying hard to smile. After a while, I pointed to the trees. "Look," I said, "look at that squirrel coming down the tree in such a hurry."

"I have seen faster squirrels," said Magda.

When a bird alighted at our entrance and started singing—just for us, I thought—I didn't mention it. I only turned halfway to look at Magda's face. She had gotten up.

"I have to go," she said. "It must have been a lot of work for you to put up this shack."

"Yes, it was," said Erika. "It took days and days to do it."

"Didn't you have anything else to do?" Magda asked. She was already outside. Only the cookies and chocolate Erika pulled out from a little hiding place made her step back into the secret house. She ate some of both, said thank-you, and left.

"You can take the flower garland and the sign," I called after her. But Magda was already well up the path, and she did not look back.

Quietly we munched our cookies. Then we just sat there, Erika in Magda's chair and I on Erika's tree stump.

It took some time for joy and beauty to enter our little house again, but when they came, they felt so good. So good. The butterfly, unappreciated by Magda, slowly sailed by again. The squirrel dashed past—stopping a

second to look at us with bright, beady eyes—
then leapt over the brook and disappeared into
the green shade.

"Come over here, Inge," said Erika. "There's
enough room for both of us on this comfortable chair."

I settled down next to her, and she took
my hand. It was wonderful to have a sister. A
twin sister to share butterflies with, and running brooks and leaping squirrels, and birds
and blades of grass and wild flowers. It felt
so good to feel as one.

Erika, My Twin

One Sunday morning Mother and Father took us for a walk through green meadows along a murmuring brook. Erika and I picked forget-me-nots for Grandmother. We caught a little frog, but we let it jump back into the water. When we came home, Grandmother had dinner ready.

I was hungry and emptied my plate so fast, I was scolded. Erika was quiet and hardly touched her food. She wasn't hungry, she said.

She was tired. I was really surprised when she didn't eat her dessert.

"Perhaps the walk was too long," said Mother. We all stared at Erika, suddenly realizing how quiet she had been.

Grandmother put a hand on Erika's forehead and said, "I think she has a fever." She had, and she was put to bed.

At first, nothing much changed. Everyone thought her chair, empty at mealtimes, would soon be occupied again. I got more attention from Grandmother, which I loved. And it made me feel special when my bed was moved into Mother and Father's bedroom. But as the days went by and Erika did not get better, I could see the worry creep into my parents' faces. Also, Grandmother did not have as many songs as usual when she went about the house doing chores.

The Doctor came every day, sometimes even twice. I was not allowed in Erika's room. It wasn't safe, they said. Sometimes I awoke in the night and turned to see my parents' bed empty. Or only Father was there, so deep asleep he did not wake up when I tried to talk to him.

Then one morning I opened my eyes to find Mother and Father bending over me. They looked at me for a long time, and they both kissed me. I looked back in silence, waiting. Mother spoke first.

"Inge," she said, "last night angels came and took Erika from us."

"I know. . . . I heard their wings," I whispered.

Father stroked my hair and said, "You are the only one now, the only one."

"The only one," I said, and a strange feeling came over me. Not so much of loneliness as of importance. The only one, I repeated in my mind, over and over. And each time I thought, *I am Inge and I am alive.*

"May I see Erika?" I asked Mother after I had dressed.

"No, dear. You can't enter that room. If you do, you might catch what made Erika so sick."

What was I to do today, I wondered. I wanted to see Erika. I was truly curious. I wanted to see what she looked like.

"Does Erika still look like me?" I asked Grandmother.

"She looks like she is asleep," Grandmother answered.

This made me even more curious. What would happen if I would climb into bed next to Erika, lie down and hold my breath? Would I look dead or would Erika look alive? I had to find out.

Against all orders I crept into the room. The curtains were drawn. My eyes had to get used to the darkness, and I was too excited to really look at Erika. Then I heard footsteps. I quickly climbed into Erika's bed, slipped under the linen sheet, and folded my hands on my chest the way Erika's were folded. The footsteps came closer. Who would find us there? Mother? Grandmother? Father? I thought my heart would burst or stop beating.

The footsteps passed. I heard another door open and shut, and the next second I found myself outside the room. Alone and alive. I trembled so much, I had to sit down.

Who are you, I asked myself. Are you Erika or are you Inge? I didn't know what to answer. Are you Inge or Erika, I asked once more. And instead of an answer, there came tears. That was how Mother found me—weeping at the door.

She sat down on the floor next to me and

cradled me in her arms. "You are all I have now," she said, "all I have."

Then Grandmother came and led us downstairs to breakfast. She put two eggs on my plate and heaped an extra portion of strawberry jam on my buttered roll. Grandmother did not say much. She looked tired, but each time our eyes met, she smiled.

After breakfast I was left alone. What does one do when one has a sister who is dead, I wondered. One goes and tells the world, I thought. The world began with Magda. I should tell her. But how? Should I call her just like I do any other morning, and then, when she puts her head out the window, simply shout, "Hello, Magda, I am Inge. Erika is dead." This didn't seem right.

Maybe I should just walk over and whisper in her ear, "I am Inge. Erika is dead." This seemed better but still not right. What would make it right?

Then I had the right idea. I would have to be in black. Black was what people wore when someone close to them died. I remembered Grandmother's huge black scarf. Standing in front of a mirror, I draped it around me. I

had to wrap it twice around myself, and still its fringe touched the floor. This made walking difficult, but step by little step I made it to the back porch.

Standing there, I felt very special. I had a dead sister. I did not know anyone else who had one. I felt important, wrapped in the black scarf.

"Magda," I called. "Magda."

She opened a window, saw me, and started to laugh.

"What is it?" she shouted. "And besides, who are you?"

"It's me," I called back. "Me. And from now on it will be always only me. Me, your best friend."

"But who are you?"

"Come to the fence," I said, "and you will see."

When we met at the fence, Magda was still laughing. "What is the funny costume for?" she wanted to know.

"It's *not* funny," I said. "I am in black because my sister is dead."

"Which one are you?" Magda asked.

For a moment I wanted to say, "I'm Erika.

Inge is dead." Instead I said nothing. Magda had stopped laughing now. She brought her face close to the fence, close to my face, focusing her eyes on the ridge of my nose.

"You are Inge," she whispered. "You are my best friend Inge. . . . Is Erika dead?"

I nodded. "Yes, your very best friend Erika is dead."

Through the fence we touched hands.

The days passed and I had to get used to being *one*. Everything was different now. At first the newness was interesting. I had Magda for myself until she and her mother went away for a visit. After that I was mostly alone.

I would put Frieda and Fat-Belly-Cross-Eye in Erika's doll buggy and push them around for hours. Both dolls are mine, I told myself. And the doll buggy is mine, too. Then one morning I carried our little bench out into the garden and set up all our dolls, Erika's and mine, in a long row, and spoke to them.

"Now, listen," I said. "You Frieda and you Lora, and you Rosemary and Leni and Fat-Belly-Cross-Eye, and you Teddy Bear and you Puck, you beautiful white dog, all of you—

listen! From now on you all belong to me. You are all *mine.*"

I sat down in front of them. I waited for a feeling of proud ownership to come over me. But nothing happened. I looked from face to face. They all were silent.

I picked up Lora and Frieda, and my arms were full. When Erika was alive, we would take one doll between us and walk her up the path together. Now Frieda, held by one arm only, dangled at my side. Her white stockings and her petticoat were dirty from touching the ground. Alone, I could not even handle two dolls at one time. What good was it to call so many dolls mine? I put Frieda and Lora back on the bench.

"You dolls really need two doll mothers," I said, and went into the house. The urge to sit beside Erika's bed was suddenly very strong. Erika, I want to think about you, really think about you, I said to myself.

When I entered our room, Mother was taking Erika's bed apart. My bed had now been moved back to its old place. Tears were streaming down Mother's cheeks. I wanted to comfort her, but I was too close to tears myself. I sat

down at the table, put my head on my folded arms and let my tears run freely.

Mother came over and sat beside me with her arm around me. Together we cried.

"I miss her," I whispered. "I miss her *so* much. She could have all my dolls *and* my cradle and all I have, if she would only come back."

"I know, darling, I know," Mother said.

"And I would always do whatever she wanted, and I would never ever say '*I wish you were dead.*'"

Now the terrible words were out. For a long time I had tried to forget them, tried to make myself believe I had never said them. But I couldn't. Prayers and good thoughts have great power, Grandmother often said. Was it possible bad thoughts had great power, too? Was it possible I had caused Erika's death? Had Mother ever heard me say those ugly words to Erika?

She must have read my thoughts, because after a little while she said, "You know, Inge, once I was very upset when I heard Erika say to you— 'I wish you were dead.'"

"She didn't mean it," I whispered.

"Neither did you," Mother said.

It was true. Sometimes I had suffered when Erika ordered me about. Sometimes I had hated her. But most of the time I had loved her. It had been wonderful to help her when she had her grand ideas, like building the secret house. Now that she was gone, I felt left over. Who would need my help now?

I raised my head from my arms and looked into Mother's face. It was red-eyed and worn. Mother put her hand on mine and said, "You are my only one now."

She had said this many times since Erika's death, but only now did I understand. I thought, *She misses Erika even more than I do.*

"Mother," I stammered, "I know I am the only one, but I promise to love you as if I was still two."

Mother nodded. "Come, we'll carry Erika's bed to the attic," she said.

The next morning I put a red *and* a blue ribbon in my hair. Mother smiled when she saw me, and we hugged each other. Now I'm helping her, I thought, and I was happy.